The Paper Plane Contest

Adapted by
Laura Baker

Learn Phonics with Peppa Pig

Phonics teaches children to read by learning the sounds of a language. They start by learning the sound for each letter or combination of letters, which helps them to break down words into sounds (**th-i-nk**). They can then blend these sounds together to read whole words ("think"). This is called sounding out and blending.

As children learn more sounds, they will meet them in lots of different combinations. With practice, they will learn to sound out and blend the sounds together to read new words.

Listen carefully as your child reads the **Learn with Peppa** stories with you. Encourage them to sound out and blend each word. If they find a word difficult, help them to sound it out. Most importantly, have fun!

Tap your finger under each dot. Drag your finger along each line. Say each sound as you do so, and then blend the sounds together to read the whole word. Sometimes, letters that are not next to each other work together to make a sound.

m a k e

Find more phonics resources, guidance and audio online:

www.learnwithpeppa.com

The Paper Plane Contest

Read the sounds
Practise sounding out and blending to read these words.

ch ie f

exploded

f l ew

n ew s p a p er

o v er

p i l o t

p l a n e

p r e t e n d e d

p r i z e

Practise the words
These words cannot be sounded out in this way. Read them with your child.

all	asked	have	here	house
into	of	said	should	some
sure	the	their	they	to
wanted	was	would	you	your

Meet the friends
This name is not as easy to sound out and blend! Read it with your child.

George

It was seven o'clock in the morning, and Daddy Pig was reading his newspaper on the lawn.

Peppa Pig asked, "Can we have some of your newspaper?"

He handed some over.

Peppa and George exploded into the house with their sheets of paper.

Mummy Pig helped them make the paper into planes.

Let's go and play with the planes!

Mummy Pig threw her plane first. It flew all the way to the field beyond the garden!

We should have a contest! If your plane flies the furthest, you win a prize.

Peppa pretended to be a pilot. Her plane glided into the field, but George's crashed like a stone into the duck pond.

George was silent.

Splash!

Peppa shrieked, "Mine flew furthest! I win!"

George burst into tears. He wanted to win, too.

Daddy Pig went inside. He looked all over the room.

He crawled under the desk and looked in his briefcase.

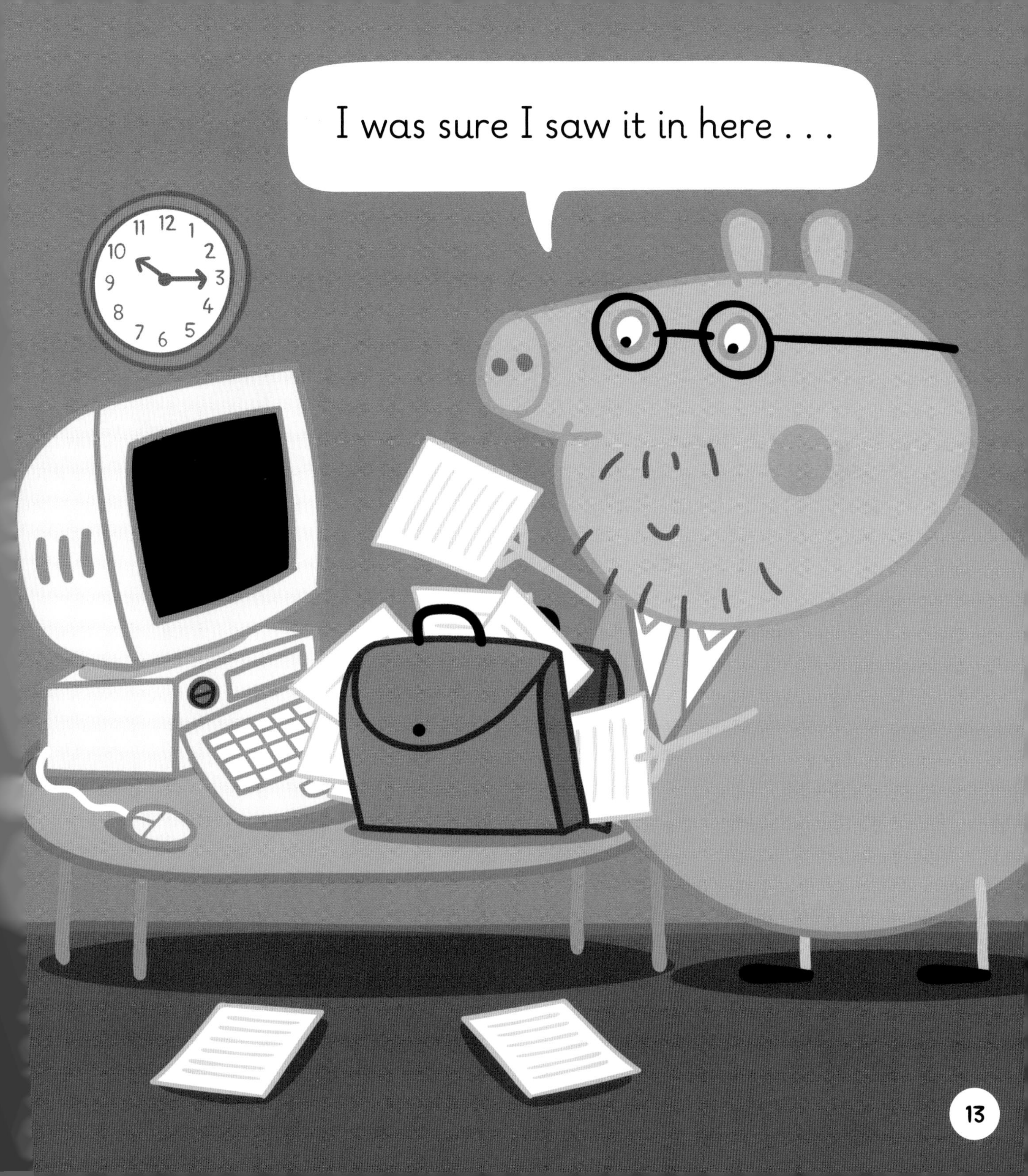
I was sure I saw it in here . . .

"Aha!" Peppa and George saw a big blue sheet behind the printer.

It would make the biggest, best plane yet!

They took it to Mummy Pig. She was the chief plane maker.

Peppa and George took their new plane to Daddy Pig with pride.

"I'm amazed!" he said.

"I hope it glides well!" Peppa said.

Daddy Pig explained, "Now, this plane belongs to all of us. We are not competing, so we all win."

Peppa nodded.

The plane flew into the clouds, and then landed in the field. Peppa and George both smiled and clapped.

They flew paper planes for the rest of the day.
They all counted to three and threw their planes.

It was fun to win, but gliding lots of planes at the same time was even better!

Have fun with Peppa Pig

 A Answer these questions about the story.

1 What type of paper did Peppa and George use to make their first paper planes?

2 Where did Mummy Pig's plane land?

3 Why did George burst into tears?

4 What was better than winning the paper plane contest?

5 Read page 15 again. Which word tells you that Mummy Pig was in charge of making paper planes?

Count to three, and then pretend to throw a paper plane in the air. What will you say as you watch your plane fly?

B

Tell me a story

You can be a storyteller! Make up a new story that starts with what you can see in this picture.

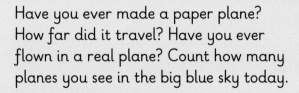

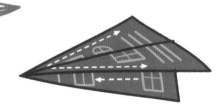

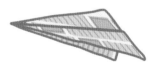

Have you ever made a paper plane? How far did it travel? Have you ever flown in a real plane? Count how many planes you see in the big blue sky today.

LADYBIRD BOOKS
UK | USA | Canada | Ireland | Australia | India | New Zealand | South Africa
Ladybird Books is part of the Penguin Random House group of companies
whose addresses can be found at global.penguinrandomhouse.com.
www.penguin.co.uk   www.puffin.co.uk   www.ladybird.co.uk

Adapted from:
Peppa Pig: Paper Planes first published by Ladybird Books Ltd 2021
Learn with Peppa Pig edition published by Ladybird Books Ltd 2023
001
© 2023 ABD Ltd/Ent. One UK Ltd/Hasbro

Adapted by Laura Baker
Phonics consultant: Charlotte Raby

Licensed by

Printed in China

The authorized representative in the EEA is Penguin Random House Ireland,
Morrison Chambers, 32 Nassau Street, Dublin D02 YH68

A CIP catalogue record for this book is available from the British Library

ISBN: 978–0–241–57652–6

All correspondence to:
Ladybird Books, Penguin Random House Children's
One Embassy Gardens, 8 Viaduct Gardens, London SW11 7BW

MIX
Paper from
responsible sources
FSC® C018179

Created and developed especially for pre-schoolers,
Learn with Peppa features a dedicated app and a fantastic range of books
to support your little ones on their early learning adventures!

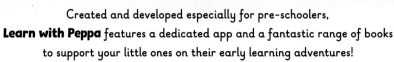

www.learnwithpeppa.com